The Wise Shoemaker of Studena

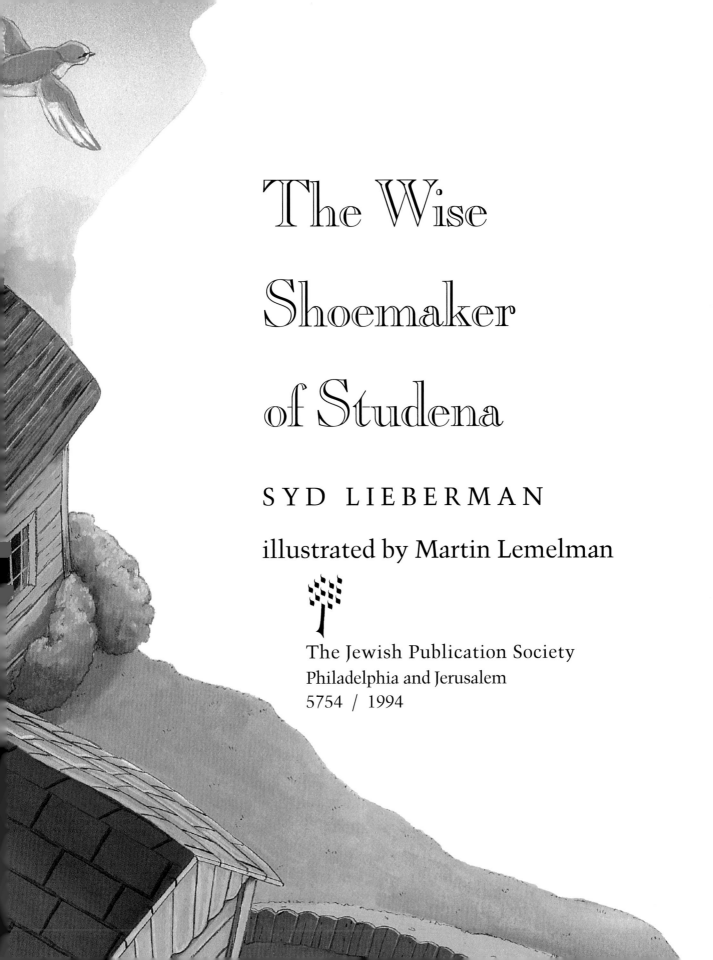

The Wise
Shoemaker
of Studena

SYD LIEBERMAN

illustrated by Martin Lemelman

The Jewish Publication Society
Philadelphia and Jerusalem
5754 / 1994

To my mother, Ruth, and my great-aunt Helen
S.L.

Happy birthday, Samuel, May you have a good life.
M.L.

Library of Congress Cataloging-in-Publication Data

Lieberman, Syd, 1994-
        The wise shoemaker of Studena / Syd Lieberman ; illustrated by
    Martin Lemelman.—1st ed.
                    p.   cm.
        Summary: When Yossi, a shoemaker respected for the wisdom of his
    advice, is invited to the wedding of the richest merchant in Budapest
    and then turned away because of his clothes, Yossi finds a ways to teach
    the merchant a lesson.
        ISBN 0-8276-0509-9
        [1. Jews—Hungary—Fiction. 2.Wisdom—Fiction.] I. Lemelman. Martin, ill.
    II. Title.
    PZ7.L61635Wi   1994
    [E]—dc20   93-43481
                                                            CIP
                                                              AC

Designed by Joanna V. Hill
Typeset in Caslon Openface and Trump Medieval

10 9 8 7 6 5 4 3 2 1

Y ossi was a shoemaker in the tiny village of Studena in the mountains of Hungary. He was skilled at mending shoes, but he was even better at giving advice. Every day the villagers would crowd into his shop, asking his opinion about one problem or another. Some days Yossi talked more than he worked.

Word of the wise shoemaker of Studena spread throughout the land. Soon rich men and even noblemen from all over Hungary began to visit Yossi. They would pull up in huge carriages, squeeze into Yossi's little shop, and fight for just a moment of his time.

And that's why Samuel, one of the richest merchants in Budapest, decided he must convince the wise shoemaker to attend his daughter's wedding.

Samuel was a man who liked to show off. He had the biggest house, the best clothes, and the largest belly of any merchant in town. "All my friends will envy me," he chuckled. "I'll be the first man in Budapest to host the wise shoemaker of Studena."

Samuel had never met Yossi, but he sent him a long letter, praising his wisdom and begging him to come to Budapest for the wedding. The wise shoemaker was delighted. He had never seen Budapest, and he had always dreamed of going there.

Yossi closed his shop immediately and ran home to tell his wife the good news. "But what will you wear to such a wedding?" asked the wife. "Even your best clothes aren't good enough."

Yossi simply smiled. "Why should I worry about what I wear? A goat has a beard, but that doesn't make him a rabbi."

It was a long trip to Budapest, but Yossi was so excited he hardly noticed the bumpy road. The bustling city turned out to be even grander than he had imagined. The people wore splendid clothes. The buildings towered above him. They looked like palaces.

As he walked, Yossi craned his neck in all directions. Suddenly, he tripped on the cobblestone street and fell into a mud puddle. When he got up, Yossi was covered with mud and found that one of his sleeves had ripped. "What would my wife say about my clothes now?" the shoemaker muttered to himself. "I will have to apologize to Samuel. But when I explain, he will certainly understand."

At the door of his fine house, Samuel was greeting guests. As he peered down the street, he saw a man approaching dressed in ripped and muddy clothes. Samuel frowned. "That man's a beggar. I don't want any beggars at my daughter's fine wedding."

Before Yossi could squeeze even a word out, Samuel shouted, "Away with you! My daughter is getting married today. I'm expecting a very important man soon—the wisest man in all the land—and I don't want him to see any beggars here!" With that, Samuel took Yossi by the shoulders, spun him around, and pushed him out into the street.

"Hmm," Yossi thought to himself, "is this the man who says he loves wisdom? He's not very smart; I will have to teach him a lesson." Immediately, Yossi hurried off to the mansion of a nobleman who had visited him in Studena the week before.

When the nobleman heard Yossi's story, he agreed to help. Opening the door to his large closet, he invited Yossi to borrow any of his finest clothes. The showmaker changed into purple velvet pants and a white Italian silk shirt with ruffles in the front. He pulled brown leather boots up to his knees and donned a gold and silver brocade coat. The nobleman perched a large black silk hat on Yossi's head. Then Yossi took the man's walking stick with a magnificent gold knob, and off he strode to the wedding.

This time, when Samuel saw Yossi coming, he thought, "That must be the shoemaker. Look how beautifully he's dressed. I knew he was a great man." Samuel greeted him with the greatest respect. He took the shoemaker by the hand and proudly introduced him to all his guests. After the wedding ceremony, Samuel seated Yossi in a place of honor, right next to the bride and groom.

Wine was served, and Samuel rose to toast the new couple. "To your health and happiness." Everyone stood and drank a glass of wine. That is, everyone but Yossi. The shoemaker just stood there, holding the glass and smiling at everyone.

The whole crowd leaned toward him, expecting that the wise shoemaker would say something wonderful. But Yossi didn't say anything. He simply pulled his purple trousers away from his body and poured the wine down his pants.

Some people laughed and some whispered in amazement. But no one said a word to Yossi, for, after all, he was the wise shoemaker of Studena.

The rest of the meal continued in the same way. Yossi poured chicken soup into his boot and swished it around. He smeared carrots down one of his arms and sauerkraut up the other.

He pushed potatoes into his shirt and tossed peas into his hat. He very carefully placed cabbage balls into one of his coat pockets and chicken paprikash into the other. Then he merrily squashed them.

The guests were astonished. No one knew what to say or do. Of couse, some of the children tried to imitate Yossi, but their parents didn't let them get very far.

When dessert was served, Yossi held up a piece of apple strudel, grinned, and mashed the pastry against his chest.

Finally, Samuel had had enought. He leaped to his feet. "What are you doing?" he shouted. "I invited you here to honor my daughter. You are known for your wisdom. But instead of speaking wisely or teaching us anything, you have been acting like a madman."

"Oh," said Yossi, looking startled, "but I have been teaching you ever since the meal began. You see, I was the man you threw out earlier. You drove me off because you thought I was a beggar. And you thought that simply because of the way I was dressed. But when I returned dressed in the clothes of a rich man, you treated me with honor and respect.

"It seems you didn't really want me here at all. You just wanted my clothes. And so I am feeding them." And with that he poured a cup of tea into his pocket and patted it fondly. "Drink well, my coat," he said as he strolled out the door.

The next day, back at home, Yossi sat nibbling his simple breakfast and thinking about the wedding. "So," said his wife as she entered, sweeping the floor, "was I right about your clothes?"

Yossi laughed, rose, and took the broom out of her hand. He examined it seriously at arm's length and then danced with it a step or two.

"You know," he said with a wink, "even this broom would look good if you dressed it up. Fools see people's clothes; the wise see their souls."